To Kedarnath Neupane, the Principal of Kanya
Mandir Secondary School, who encouraged me
to publish my poems for children
— D. L. S.

In loving memory of Aji
— S. M.

The Great Hairy Khyaa

Original text: Durga Lal Shrestha
Illustrator: Suman Maharjan
Translated from Nepal Bhasa

Who's down there?

The Great Hairy Khyaa!

Why are you here?

For the feast!

What feast?

Lakhamari feast!

Any
good?

Very good!

Had enough?

NEVER!!

No! I am scared
to go where it's dark.

Ma,

is this the khyaa
that scares me so?

Won't it pounce on us?
Won't it pull our legs?
Ma,
is this the khyaa
that scares me so?

When it stands in the dark, it covers ground and sky. Just watching it stretch, makes my temples fry.!

But it disappears as soon as the lights come on...

It was just **here**

and now it's **gone!**

Ma, is this the khyaa that scares me so?

Where's Rag Ball Khyaa?
Where's the Great Hairy One?

Nowhere to be seen when light has won!

What kind of khyaa is afraid of light?

But what about me, who's such an easy bite?

Ma, is this the khyaa that scares me so?

रज्या: ग्याः

छन् सु बल ?
धाँ ब्याः

ब याइबल ?
बस् नःबल

ब बस् ?
लाछामनि बस्

लाछामनि साइला ?
साः साः

डलिं गाइला ?
मगाः

यः जिला यः
ब्रूबाय् बन यः

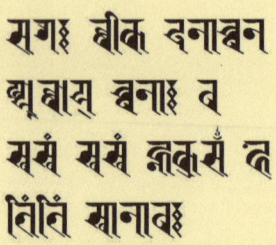

यः मां जिम ब्यानाबंब्म
व द ब्यना यः ?

दसब् वि बं नुनि यः वि बं
जि नं सिब् यः

यः मां जिम ब्यानाबंब्म
व द ब्यना यः ?

सगः बीब् दनाब्न
ब्रूबाय् ब्नाः व
सम्मं सम्मं ब्रब्रसैं व
निनि ब्यानाबः

मन ब्याकः सयीं वबा
ब्नि मद बाः
मद् नब्निनि दुब्म
यबायुश्रीब्म यः
ब्बायुश्रीब्म यः

यः मां जिम ब्यानाबंब्म
व द ब्यना यः ?

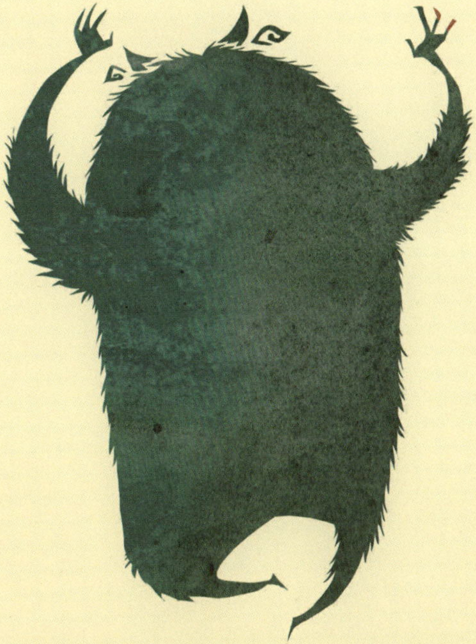

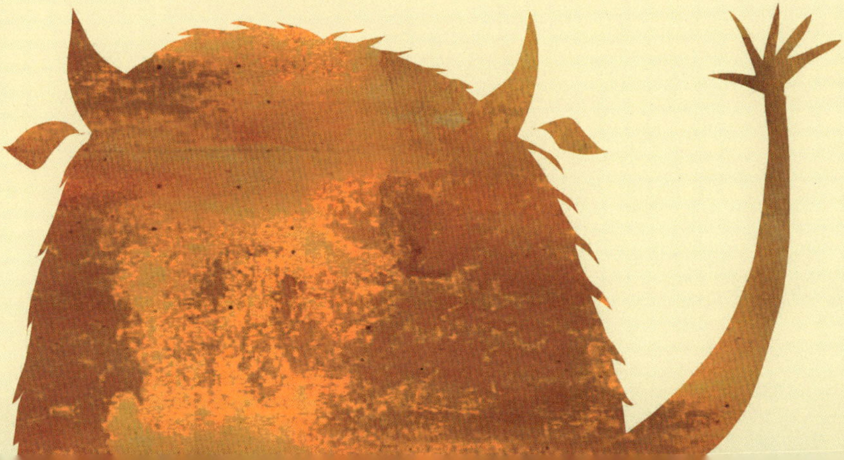

रञ्ज्जना लिपि Ranjana Script

माआखः Vowels

अ	अः	आ	आः	इ	ई	उ	ऊ	ऋ	ॠ	ऌ	ॡ	ए	ऐ	ओ	औ	अँ	अं	अय्	आय्	एय्
a	a-h	aa	aa-h	i	ee	u	oo	ri	ree	lri	lree	e	ai	o	au	añ	aṃ	ay	aay	ey

बाआखः Consonants

क	ख	ग	घ	ङ	ङ्ह	च	छ	ज	झ	ञ	ट	ठ	ड	ढ	ण	त	थ	द	ध	न	न्ह
ka	kha	ga	gha	ṅa	ṅha	cha	chha	ja	jha	ña	ṭa	ṭha	ḍa	ḍha	ṇa	ta	tha	da	dha	na	nha

प	फ	ब	भ	म	म्ह	य	ह्य	र	ऱ्ह	ल	ल्ह	व	व्ह	श	ष	स	ह	क्ष	त्र	ज्ञ
pa	pha	ba	bha	ma	mha	ya	hya	ra	rha	la	lha	wa	wha	sha	ṣa	sa	ha	kṣa	tra	gya

त्याः Numbers

०	१	२	३	४	५	६	७	८	९
0	1	2	3	4	5	6	7	8	9

🔍 Find the first letter of your name in Ranjana script.

✏️ Practice writing it.

🔍 Find **ख्याः** in the poem in Ranjana Lipi on the previous pages.

✏️ Try writing it yourself.

khyaa = (kh) + (ya) + (aa) + (a-h)

? What do these words in Nepal Bhasa mean?

Khyaa: a mischievous spirit or ghost

Lakhamari: a crunchy Newar pastry with icing

✎ Use the above Nepal Bhasa words to make sentences.

First published in Nepal in 2018 by Safu
Damodar Marg, Lalitpur
qcbookshop.com

© 2018 by The Asia Foundation
Original text copyright © Durga Lal Shrestha
Illustration copyright © 2018 by Suman Maharjan
Originally sung in *Culiciyā Caṃ Caṃ* (1991)

All rights reserved.
26 25 24 23 22 21 20 19 18   1 2 3 4 5

ISBN 978-9937-9258-9-1
Writer: Durga Lal Shrestha
Illustrator: Suman Maharjan
English translation: Mahendra Man Singh
Editor: Muna Gurung
Designer: Dishebh Shrestha
Art Director: Sharareh Bajracharya

Published as part of
Safu Language Series: Nepal Bhasa Children's Books

The Asia Foundation

This book was created with the generous support of The Asia Foundation's Books for Asia program. For more information and to access a digital version of this and many more books, please visit: letsreadasia.org or download the Let's Read! app from the Google Play Store.

सृजनालय SRIJANALAYA

Srijanalaya, which produced this book, is an NGO based in Nepal that creates safe spaces for learning through the arts. For more information, visit srijanalaya.org.

Some rights reserved. No part of this publication may be reproduced, stored in a retrieval system or transmitted in any form or by any means, electronic, mechanical or photocopying, recording, or otherwise for commercial purposes without the prior permission of The Asia Foundation.

This book is licensed under a Creative Commons Attribution-NonCommercial 4.0 International License.

About the Author

Durga Lal Shrestha is a poet and lyricist of Nepal Bhasa and Nepali. As a teacher of Nepal Bhasa at Kanya Mandir Higher Secondary School from the 1950s to the 1980s, he created songs to inspire children to express themselves in their mother tongue. The collections of his children's songs *Ciniyāmha Kisicā* (1965) continues to be a bestseller in Nepal Bhasa. Shrestha is also known as a lyricist in Nepali, and he has written popular songs including "Phūlko Aā̃khāmā". He remains an inspiration to many. He has embraced this project with great enthusiasm.

About the Illustrator

Suman Maharjan is a visual artist, animator and freelance illustrator. He loves illustrating children's picture books and has a passion for 2D character animation. He is a strong believer in DIY solutions and exploring new places. He enjoys working in different mediums, and in addition to drawing and illustrating, he has been exploring printmaking and sculpture.

Acknowledgments

This book series would not have been possible without the support of Suman and Suchita Shrestha, Durga Lal Shrestha's children, and his wife, Purnadevi Shrestha, who is always by his side. Suman Maharjan, Binita Buddhacharya, Surendra Maharjan, Ashish Shakya, Sambhaw Maharjan and Mrigaja Bajracharya each contributed their time and energy to visualize the poems. Dishebh Shrestha patiently put each of the books together. We are grateful to Mahendra Man Singh, Sharareh Bajracharya, Muna Gurung and Niranjan Kunwar for the playful English translations. Thanks to Rubin Shakya for the Nepal Bhasa edits and Rajendra Maharjan for the Nepali edits. Thank you to Amber Delahaye from Stichting Thang for holding an illustration workshop in Kathmandu. The Books for Asia team of Ritica Lacoul, Kyle Barker and Shameera Shrestha have been an essential driving force in making this project possible. Finally, a special thanks to Sharareh Bajracharya whose guidance and collaborative spirit made the production of this book series possible.

About Safu Children's Book

'Safu' means book in Nepal Bhasa. The Safu Language Series is dedicated to bringing stories from the different languages, cultures and regions of Nepal to a global audience.

SAFU

Safu Language Series: Nepal Bhasa Children's Books

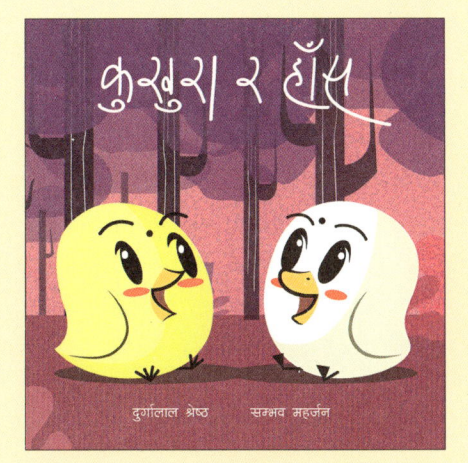

Available versions:
कुखुरा र हाँस (Nepali) NP

Available versions:
धाप्लां ख्याक् (Nepali) NP
धाप्लां ख्या: (Nepal Bhasa) NB
The Great Hairy Khyaa (English) EN

Available versions:
न्याउ न्याउ (Nepali) NP
न्याउ न्याउ (Nepal Bhasa) NB
Nyau Nyau (English) EN

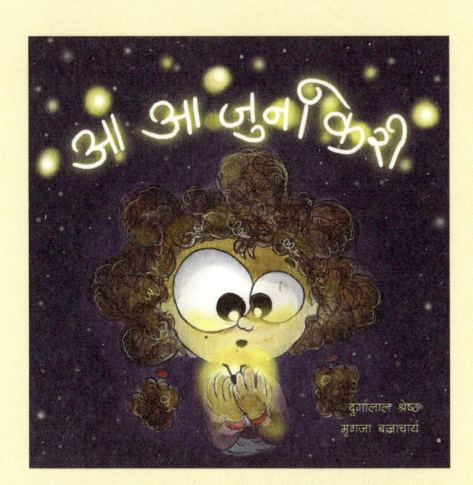

Available versions:
आ आ जुनकिरी (Nepali) NP

Available versions:
हे माकः! (Nepali) NP

Available versions:
कमिला र रोटी (Nepali) NP